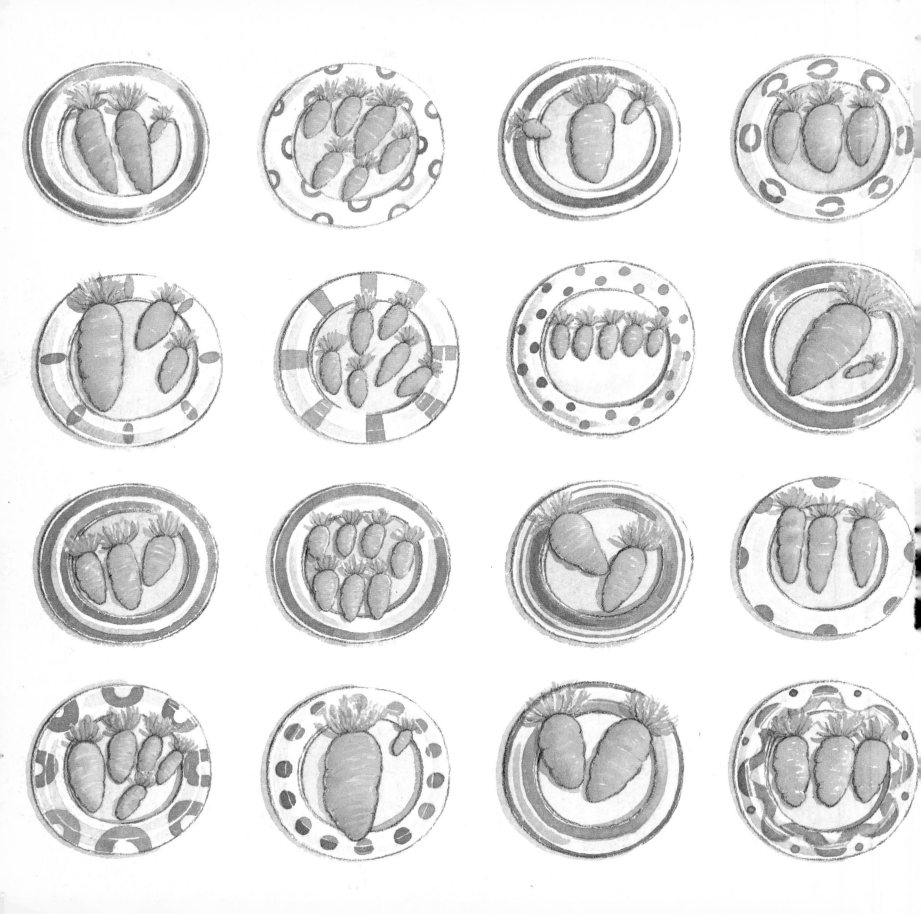

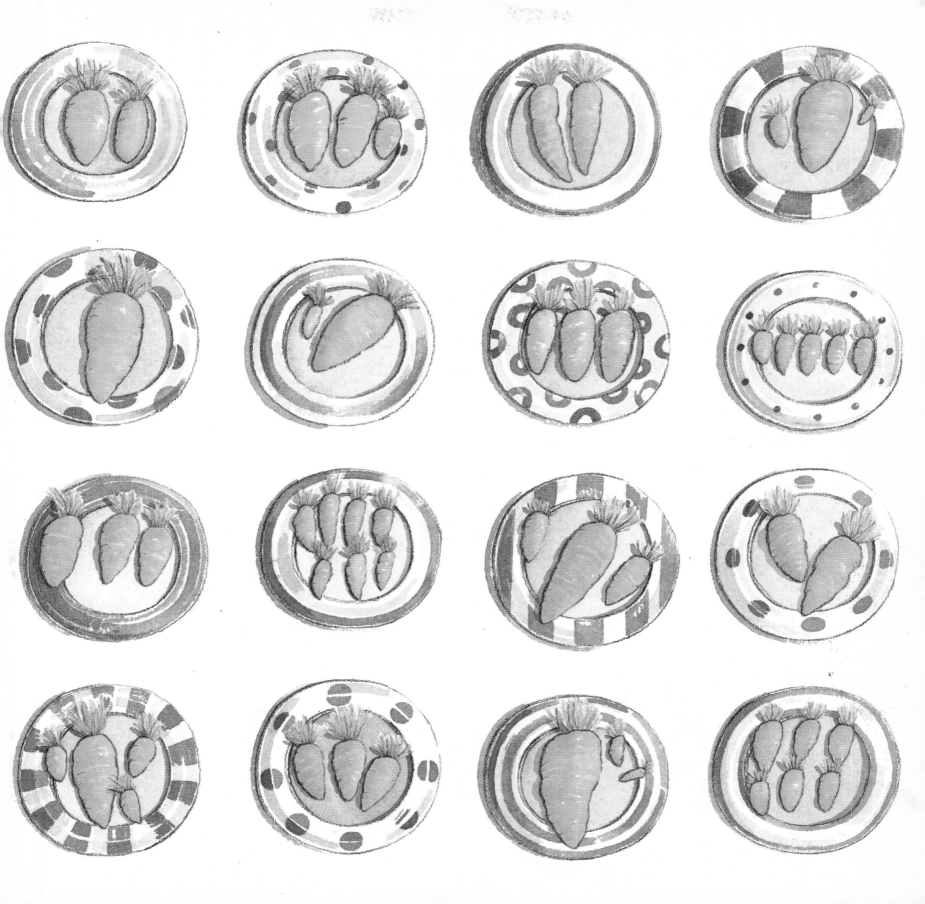

for Aaron
and Zoë

Published in 2010
by Child's Play
(International) Ltd
Ashworth Road, Bridgemead,
Swindon SN5 7YD

ISBN 978-1-84643-353-5
CLP100510CPL06103535

Printed and bound
in Heshan, China

3 5 7 9 10 8 6 4 2

Distributed in USA
by Child's Play Inc
250 Minot Avenue,
Auburn, Maine 04210
Distributed in Australia by
Child's Play Australia Pty Ltd
Unit 10/20 Narabang Way
Belrose, NSW 2085
www.childs-play.com

First published in the UK
by Puffin Books

Text and illustrations
copyright
© Penny Ives 2006
The moral right
of the author/illustrator
has been asserted

Rabbit Pie

by

Penny Ives

Child's Play ®

First, gather together your ingredients.

One game of hide-and-seek
One bath
Six pairs of pyjamas
Six cups of milk
One story
A sprinkling of soft kisses
Six large carrots

Then find **six** small rabbits...

Take off any **dirty** bits...

...and place in warm **soapy** water.

Gently scrub.

Watch **very** closely.

Fold into a soft towel

and allow to **cool down.**

Pat dry,
dust the **bottoms**

and lightly **brush** the tops.

Slowly pour in

six cups of milk.

Tuck in,
sprinkling with kisses.

Leave in a **warm** place

until **morning**.

When quite ready, serve with fresh carrots.

Sweet
Rabbit Pie!

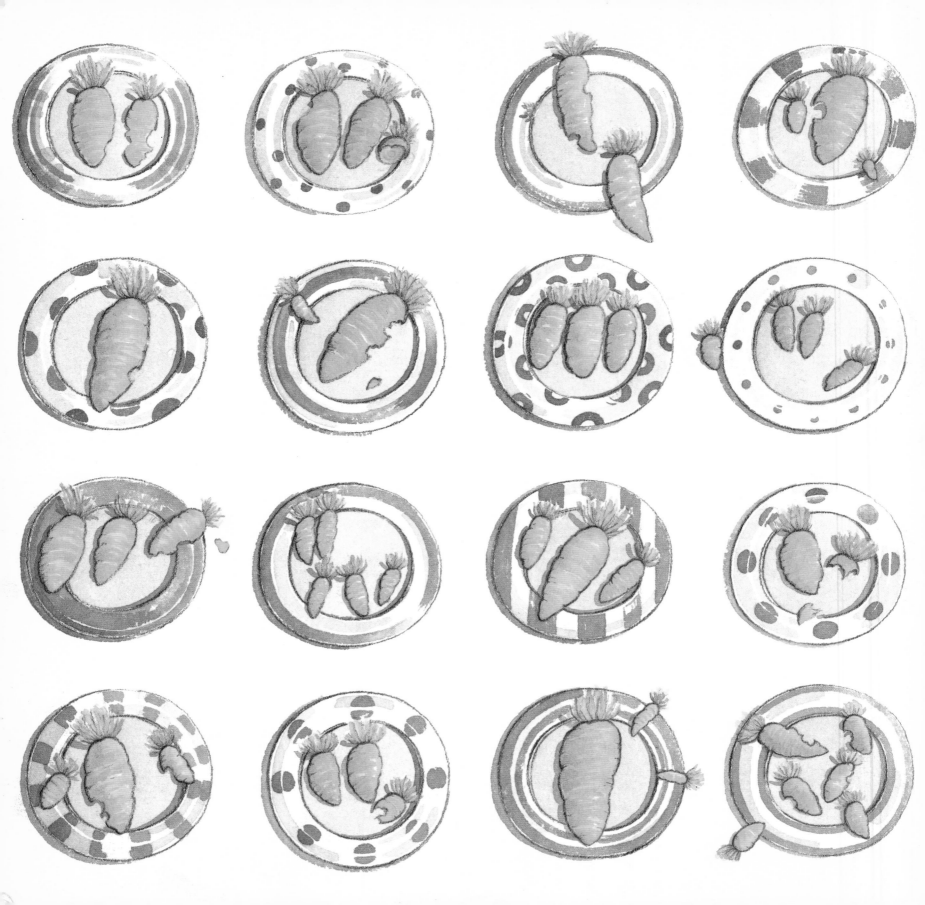

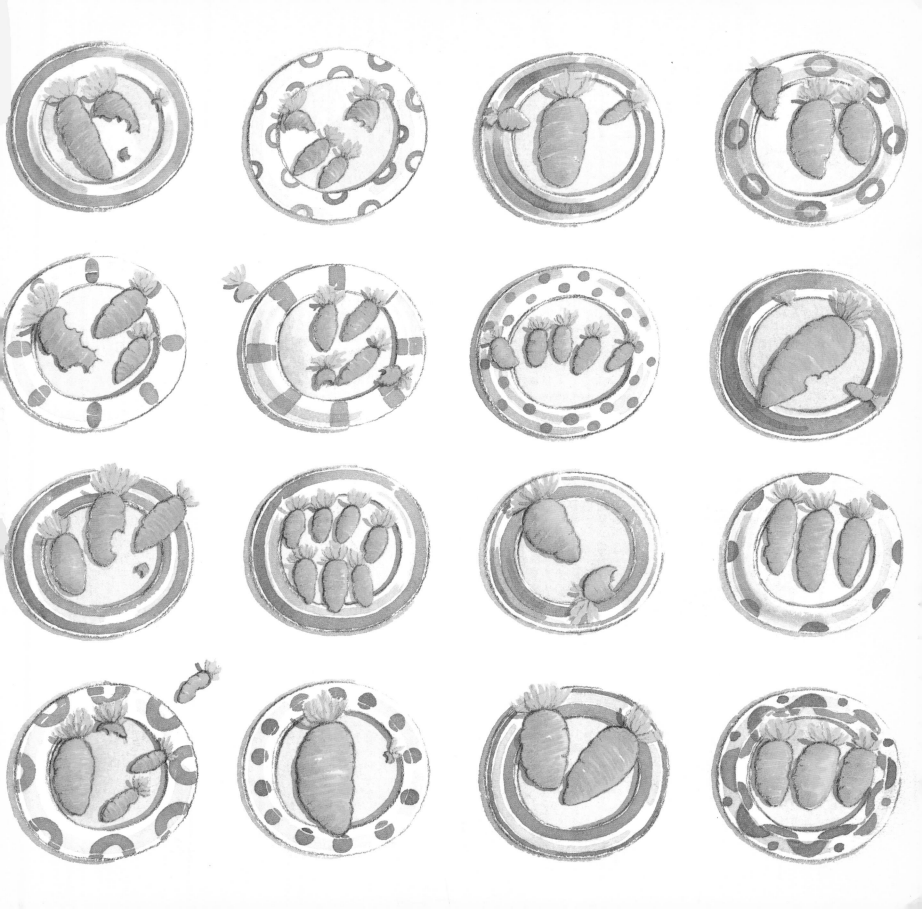